ROBIN

STARFIRE

CYBORG

RAVEN

BEAST BOY

RAVEN ROCKS!

Adapted by J. E. Bright

Based on the episodes
"Halloween" written by John Loy
"Friendship" written by Merrill Hagan
and
"Crazy Day" written by John Loy

LITTLE, BROWN AND COMPANY
New York   Boston

Little, Brown and Company

Hachette Book Group
1290 Avenue of the Americas, New York, NY 10104
Visit us at lb-kids.com

Little, Brown and Company is a division
of Hachette Book Group, Inc.
The Little, Brown name and logo are trademarks
of Hachette Book Group, Inc.

The publisher is not responsible for websites (or their content)
that are not owned by the publisher.

First Edition: October 2015

ISBN 978-0-316-37732-4

10 9 8 7 6 5 4 3 2 1

RRD-C

Printed in the United States of America

CONTENTS

CHAPTER

In the ominous, flickering glow of the Titans Tower living room, Raven got ready.

It is time, she thought solemnly as she pulled on layers of material. *I must don the ceremonial garb. Tonight, darkness shall creep over the land. Terror will walk the streets. Children will shriek in fear.* Her eyes narrowed as she gathered her determination. *Tonight we will face our greatest demons.*

Now that she was in the appropriate dress, Raven stepped out of the shadows.

She wore a bright pink costume of the winged horse Sparkleface from her favorite

TV show, *Pretty, Pretty Pegasus*,. "Happy Hallow-een!" she cheered, and snapped her fingers.

In a flash of dark magic, Raven decorated the room for the creepy holiday. Black and orange streamers and plastic spiders festooned the room, along with dangling skeletons.

Her fellow Teen Titans barely reacted. They were sitting on the couch, watching TV. Cyborg shrugged his metallic shoulders. Beast Boy's eyelids drooped. Starfire slumped deeper into the sofa. "Meh," mumbled Robin.

"That's it?" Raven protested. "Come on, guys. Halloween!" She hovered beside Starfire. "Look!" She gasped, holding out a tissue-paper ghost on a string. "A scary ghost! *Wooo!*"

"Your paper ghost is well made, Raven," said Starfire, "but not scary."

"Grr!" growled Raven. She jammed a glowing pumpkin carved like her demon father, Trigon, in front of Robin's and Cyborg's faces. "I'm a jack-o'-lantern!"

"What a waste of good produce," said Robin.

Raven grimaced. "Who wants candy?" she asked hopefully. "We can get bags of it tonight!"

"If we want candy," replied Cyborg, crossing his arms, "we'll go buy some."

Raven bobbed in front of Beast Boy, blocking his view. "I know for a fact you love costumes."

Beast Boy smiled at her, gesturing at his uniform. "We wear costumes every day."

"What's going on, guys?" demanded Raven, putting her fists on her hips. "Halloween is our favorite holiday."

Robin raised a single gloved finger. "*Was* our favorite holiday," he corrected her.

"But every year we always have so much fun," Raven argued.

Starfire shook her head. "Do you not remember last year, Raven?"

Last year, the Titans all had dressed in scary costumes and went out trick-or-treating in Jump City. When they returned to the Tower that evening, they all felt pukey.

"Why did I eat all that candy?" Robin groaned.

Cyborg clutched his tummy. He was at the breaking point.

Beast Boy was entirely the wrong shade of green. What had happened next was not pretty....

CHAPTER 2

Remembering that wretched event from last year, Cyborg, Starfire, Robin, and Beast Boy all felt a little ill again.

"That's what happens when you eat the candy with the wrappers still on," scolded Raven.

Starfire shook her head. "We are sorry,

Raven, but there will be no hallowing this ween."

"Why do you care so much anyway?" asked Robin.

Raven rose up from the floor, surrounded by a furious dark glow. "Because I'm half demon," she thundered. "That's like being a Pilgrim on Thanksgiving!" She let her powers subside. "You know, I like doing scary stuff with you guys."

"We did, too," explained Cyborg. "The best part of Halloween is being scared. It just doesn't scare us anymore."

"Yeah, I'm a grown man now, doing grown-man business," agreed Beast Boy. "I don't have time to be scared."

Raven couldn't believe her teammates were done with Halloween's thrills and chills. She held a flashlight under her face to make herself look creepy. "*Wooo...*" she moaned ghoulishly. "*Woooooo...*"

Beast Boy, Robin, Starfire, and Cyborg stared at her. They blinked in unison.

"*Woooo...*" Raven tried again.

"Are you done?" asked Robin.

"*Woo*," said Raven.

Her teammates focused back on the TV.

Raven sighed in frustration and headed to her room.

When she was alone in her private sanctum, Raven floated among her belongings, feeling cranky. "Don't have time to get scared," she groused. "What kind of people *are* they?"

Raven glowered at her spell table, staring at her laboratory and casting equipment. Then she smiled, struck with an idea.

With a flick of her hand, Raven conjured up a creepy, ancient book. It groaned as she cracked it open, and ghostly howls echoed within her room as she flipped through its dusty pages.

"Maybe to get them into the Halloween spirit," Raven said, "I need a little help from *the* Halloween Spirit."

CHAPTER 3

Raven clapped her hands and a hollow pumpkin popped into existence, floating in front of her. She opened it by its stem and began tossing in ingredients. "One witch's eye," she said, "a strand of spiderweb, and three candy corns—" Before Raven dropped in the sweets, she munched on one. "*Two* candy corns."

As her makeshift cauldron bubbled and boiled, Raven intoned, *"Azarath Metrion Zinthos!"*

A wriggling, furiously howling entity with fiery eyes appeared and was sucked down into the pumpkin. Raven jammed the stemmed top shut, trapping the being inside.

The entirety of Titans Tower flashed. The Halloween Spirit was present.

Down in the living room, Robin was alone on the couch. Unblinking, he stared at the TV. A tissue-paper ghost slowly lowered down on a string and dangled beside his head.

Robin gave it a side-eyed glance. "Paper ghost!" he screeched in surprising terror.

Raven smiled. Her spirit-powered pumpkin floated behind her.

Starfire flew full-speed into the living

room. "What is all the locomotion, Robin?" she cried. "Are you—" She spotted a plastic skeleton hanging nearby and screamed, falling backward with her eyes wide.

Alarmed, Cyborg and Beast Boy tumbled into the room.

Cyborg put his fists on his hips. "I hope there's a good reason you're all screaming."

"Yeah," added Beast Boy. "It's really—"

Both of the guys' eyes bugged out when they saw a robot zombie hand wiggle its fingers on the coffee table. They shrieked and dove onto the couch with Robin and Starfire, huddling with them in horror. The four terrified Titans pointed at various decorations, screaming at everything.

Watching her teammates lose their minds,

Raven rubbed her hands together gleefully. "Finally," she said, "it's starting to feel like Halloween." She shouted over the screaming, "Guys!"

Still huddled together, the other Titans peered up at Raven.

"Yeah?" asked Beast Boy, his voice shaking.

Raven turned on a flashlight underneath her chin. It lit up her face with spooky shadows. "Boo," she said.

Her teammates shrieked in absolute terror. Beast Boy turned into a hedgehog. His spines shredded the top of his uniform.

Raven clicked off the flashlight. "Relax," she said. "It's just me."

Starfire wiped her brow. "Oh, thank the goodness," she said, breathing raggedly.

Beast Boy stood in front of Raven, showing her his bare green torso. "You scared me shirtless!"

"What's going on?" asked Raven. "I thought you weren't scared of Halloween."

"I thought so, too," replied Cyborg. He spotted a fake arachnid on the couch and shuddered. "But every time I see a plastic spider I want to cry."

Robin hugged himself in his own arms. "Why are we suddenly scared of everything?"

"Oh no!" squeaked Starfire. She peered at the Titans' computer monitor, which was flashing softly. "We have the trouble." She pulled up the exterior camera view of the front door.

A bunch of little kids in costumes skipped up the front walk. They held bags and plastic pumpkins.

"Oooh," Raven whispered, making her voice spooky. "Trick-or-treaters."

"What do they want?" shrieked Robin.

CHAPTER 4

Raven stared at her teammates solemnly.

"They want," she moaned, "tricks or treats."

"Nooo…" sobbed Beast Boy.

"Don't let them in," Cyborg gasped.

Robin pushed Starfire out of the way and gaped at the computer monitor. "Code red!" he barked. "I repeat: code red! Go into lockdown! Now!" He jammed his finger down on a button on the console.

The defenses around Titans Tower activated. Alarms blared. Metal gates slammed down over the windows. Spikes sprung out on all edges. Atop the front door, dozens of massive weapons took aim at the intruders.

Seeing the hi-tech cannons pointed at them, the trick-or-treaters fled.

"We've secured the perimeter," Robin declared. "Now we have to secure the interior!" He raised a gloved fist. "Titans, go!"

In a blur, Robin, Starfire, Cyborg, and Beast Boy zoomed around the inside of their headquarters, ripping down all the Halloween decorations. They shredded the paper ghosts, dismembered the skeletons, smashed plastic bugs and bats, and tossed zombie parts into the garbage. When all the creepy stuff was destroyed, they focused on Raven's glowing pumpkin.

"Oh no! Stop, guys!" cried Raven. "Not the pumpkin!" She lunged to block her teammates, but she had reacted too late.

Starfire and Cyborg obliterated it with blasts of violent energy.

With a chilling howl, the Halloween Spirit rose up from the smashed gourd. Now released from its prison, it expanded in fury, filling the living room.

The Teen Titans—including Raven—tumbled backward in shock and horror.

Shrieking in rage, the powerful specter swooped around the room and then shot out of the Tower, heading toward Jump City across the harbor.

Raven shook her head in dismay. "You guys just released the Halloween Spirit."

"The what?" asked Beast Boy.

"The Halloween Spirit," replied Raven. "Behold!" With a flourish of her hand, she conjured up her spell book in front of her.

Her teammates gasped in fear at the sudden appearance.

Raven rolled her eyes. "It's just a book," she said. "Relax."

CHAPTER 5

Raven read from her ancient tome, "'Since the dawn of time, the Halloween Spirit terrorized the land, feeding on the fear of children.'" When she flipped the page, the scary illustration of the specter made her teammates cringe and whimper.

"Get it together," she scolded her friends. Raven kept reading. "'Finally, the people had enough. They would fight fear with fear, and the Halloween Spirit was banished. From their victory, our Halloween traditions were born.'"

She closed the heavy covers of the book, and it vanished in a poof.

"We can stop it again!" explained Raven. "But we're going to need three things: costumes, jack-o'-lanterns, and candy. Let's do it."

As funky music blasted through the Tower, the Teen Titans ran around pulling together costumes and getting dressed up. By the time the song ended, they were ready for Halloween. They lined up in the living room.

Raven inspected her costumed friends. Robin was dressed as a vampire. Cyborg was a pirate. Beast Boy wore a red demon costume.

Starfire was a fairy princess, complete with a tiara.

Raven nodded. "You guys look... *spooktacular*."

Starfire looked at Robin. Robin looked at Cyborg. Cyborg looked at Beast Boy. Beast Boy looked at Starfire. They all yelped, scared by one another's costumes.

Raven pulled out an armful of chunky pumpkins. She tossed them at her teammates, who cowered away in fear. "Carve them!" demanded Raven.

On command, Robin flipped into the air and attacked his pumpkin with a blizzard of karate chops and kicks.

Starfire blasted a pumpkin with a flash of sizzling power from her eyes.

Cyborg aimed the laser in his mechanical arm at a pumpkin, cutting it up with hot light.

Beast Boy transformed into a cat and slashed his pumpkin with sharp claws.

The carved pumpkins fell into an orderly line across from the Titans. Raven examined their creations.

Robin's jack-o'-lantern had a traditional design, with a gap-toothed grin. "Classic," Raven declared.

Starfire's pumpkin had an evil smile and pointy eyebrows. "Scary," said Raven.

Beast Boy's design was a bit haphazard, with off-center eyes. "Competent," said Raven.

Cyborg's pumpkin had an intricately carved baby face. Raven smiled at it. "Aw, cute."

Then Raven hovered in front of the pumpkins, opening her arms. "What do you guys think?" she asked.

They all blinked at the pumpkins. Then they shrieked in horror at their scary handiwork.

Raven nodded, pleased. "Now we just need candy. Lots of it."

"Where are we going to get candy at this hour?" asked Cyborg.

The answer was obvious. They headed into Jump City and went door to door, trick-or-treating!

The Teen Titans had collected bags of candy. They gave one another high fives.

But soon the Halloween Spirit rose above Jump City, using its mystical powers to awaken monsters. Skeletons, zombies, vampires, ghouls, and other lumbering beasts crawled out of the earth. The monsters shook off their dirt and wandered the streets, terrifying trick-or-treaters and chasing the screaming citizens through the city.

The Teen Titans watched the rampage, their eyes wide with horror.

"What were we thinking?" cried Robin, trembling. "We're too scared to fight that thing!"

"I'm too scared to even look at you!" Beast Boy told Cyborg, shielding his eyes.

"I'm too scared to even look at *you*!" Cyborg replied. He peeked at Beast Boy and shrieked.

Raven heaved a deep sigh. "The only

reason you're scared is because I cast a spell to put you back in the Halloween spirit," she admitted.

"Why would you do that?" asked Starfire.

"Because Halloween was the one day of the year we all looked forward to," explained Raven. "Pumpkin carving, trick or treating, haunted houses. I was just trying to get all that back." She bowed her head, feeling sorry. "Instead, I ruined Halloween."

CHAPTER 6

Robin put his hand on Raven's shoulder.
"Are you kidding?" he asked. "Even though I've had to change my pants three times, we've had a blast doing Halloween stuff with you."

"Yeah," agreed Beast Boy. "I guess we just forgot how much fun being scared could be."

"It's like being a little kid again!" added Cyborg.

Raven peered up at her friends. "Really?" she asked.

Raven's teammates gathered around her, nodding and smiling.

Raven held up a fist. "Then let's take down the Halloween Spirit."

Robin, Beast Boy, Cyborg, and Starfire reacted in terror, shrinking back and cowering.

"Oh no," Robin whimpered. "Weren't you listening to us? We're way too scared for that."

"Don't worry," said Raven. "You just need a little extra pep in your step to help you overcome that fear." She held up her overflowing bag of candy. "Eat it," she instructed.

The Teen Titans gobbled down as much candy as they could. At least they remembered to unwrap the treats this year!

As they ate, the heroes stood taller and looked healthier and less scared.

Cyborg flexed his muscular arm. "I've got so much energy!" he announced.

"I feel like my heart's on fire!" declared Beast Boy.

Robin put his fists on his hips. "Me too!"

Starfire raised her hands in the air and screamed in jubilation.

Raven passed around bowls of garden vegetables. "Now eat a salad to balance it out," she said.

The Teen Titans stood eating their salads with forks.

"This also gives me energy," said Cyborg. His mechanical eye glowed brightly.

Beast Boy crunched and swallowed. "These croutons are wonderful."

"Mmm," murmured Robin. "Nutritious."

Starfire waved her hands in the air and hollered in sheer exuberance.

The Halloween Spirit's monsters continued to terrorize Jump City.

Raven gathered her teammates together in a huddle. "Now the only way to get to the Halloween Spirit is to use our costumes to scare a path to it," she explained. "Teen Titans, go!"

The heroes leaped into action. They jumped out at monsters, surprising them from behind walls, benches, and mailboxes.

"Boo!" shouted Robin, ambushing a vampire. It turned to dust.

"Booyah!" Cyborg hollered at a zombie. It fell to pieces.

Beast Boy sprang up at a ghoul and hollered, "Booo!" It faded out of existence.

Starfire surprised a skeleton with an alien noise that sounded somewhat like *boo*. Its bones collapsed in a heap.

Soon the Teen Titans had defeated all the monsters. They reached the Halloween Spirit. It loomed above Jump City, its eyes glowing with terrifying fire.

The Titans trembled in front of it, too scared to attack.

"Jack-o'-lanterns," said Raven. She clapped. In a flash, carved pumpkins appeared in each Titan's hands.

"Light them up!" shouted Raven. She clapped again, and all the jack-o'-lanterns glowed brighter and brighter.

The Teen Titans raised their jack-o'-lanterns, pointing the blazing faces at the Halloween Spirit. Brilliant light shot from the pumpkins' eyes, merging together to form an awesome beam of pure energy.

The blast of power shot toward the Halloween Spirit and zapped it. The specter shuddered in pain.

Raven rolled another pumpkin directly under the Halloween Spirit. As the beams of power continued to weaken the spirit, the new pumpkin drew the Halloween Spirit down into itself. In a burst, the Halloween Spirit became trapped inside, creating a terrifying jack-o'-lantern face on the pumpkin.

The citizens of Jump City cheered, and the Teen Titans jumped up and down in celebration.

"Best Halloween ever!" screamed Beast Boy.

"Let's do it again next year!" added Cyborg.

Raven hovered beside her happy friends. "Thanks for spending Halloween with me, guys," she said. "There's just one last thing...."

"What?" asked Robin.

Raven flicked on a flashlight under her chin, casting her face in eerie shadows. "Boo," she said.

Starfire, Cyborg, Robin, and Beast Boy scrambled away, screaming in fear.

Raven smiled. "I love Halloween."

CHAPTER 1

The adorable winged horses Sparkleface and Butterbean were chatting pleasantly in the shimmering, colorful Cotton Candy Grove.

"Oh no, Sparkleface," said Butterbean. "The cotton candy isn't growing because there hasn't been a shower in weeks."

Sparkleface tilted her pink head in

confusion. "But it rained just yesterday, Butterbean."

"Not that kind of shower, silly," replied Butterbean. "It needs a shower of compliments!"

Sparkleface laughed. "Of course it does," she said. She leaned over to whisper to the wispy mounds of spun sugar. "You're the most amazing cotton candy ever!"

"And so delicious, too," added Butterbean. "Yum, yum, yum!"

Under their loving attention, the cotton candy glowed and grew larger, basking in their kind words.

"Look," cheered Sparkleface. "It's working!"

Suddenly, the harsh sounds of thumping drums echoed throughout the grove. The cotton candy withered and drooped.

"Oh no!" cried Sparkleface. "That noise is ruining the cotton candy's natural fluffiness."

Butterbean twitched her yellow ears as she listened. "It's coming from the unicorns," she realized.

They met each other's eyes with matching worried looks.

Raven hovered above the sidewalk in Jump City as she watched her favorite TV show, *Pretty, Pretty Pegasus*, in the big window of a department store. Her eyes had the same worried look as Butterbean and Sparkleface on the TV screen. "The unicorns sound like trouble," muttered Raven.

"Hey, Raven," called Robin behind her.

"What?" asked Raven, turning around. A few feet away, her Teen Titans teammates were battling a chunky villain named Control Freak. Even though Control Freak was holding up his powerful remote-control device, the Titans were definitely winning.

"You want to get in on the fun?" asked Robin as he kicked the villain.

"It's just Control Freak," replied Raven. "I'm good."

Robin shrugged. "It's your loss," he said. He took out his bo staff and whacked Control Freak with it. The smack knocked the villain over, and Control Freak rolled against the department store wall.

Upside down, Control Freak noticed the show Raven was watching. "Oooh," he said. "Is this a new episode of *Pretty, Pretty Pegasus*?"

"Yeah," answered Raven. "The unicorns are playing their music too loud and ruining all the cotton candy."

Control Freak waggled his legs, trying to get up. "Sounds like a doozy of a problem," he said. "But there's nothing friendship can't fix."

"That's what I love about the show," said Raven. "It has such good messages."

Control Freak managed to roll himself right side up. "It's nice to see a cartoon where the characters don't have to solve every problem through violence."

CHAPTER 2

Cyborg grabbed Control Freak's thick leg and yanked him into the air. "You like TV so much, here's a rerun of your last beat-down!" shouted Cyborg. He slammed him against the pavement. *"Shablamo!"*

Control Freak yelped.

Before the villain could recover, Beast Boy turned into a gorilla and jumped up and down on him with his four-hundred-pound body. "Yo," he said, "how do I turn down the volume on your cries of pain, fool? *Kaboom!*"

"Ow," gasped Control Freak. "Ow. Ow!"

Starfire blasted the orange-haired bad guy with energy beams from her eyes. "I do not know how to make the television reference!" she yelled.

Control Freak slammed back into the department store wall again. He managed to hold up his remote control.

"Put down the remote, Control Freak," ordered Robin. "Haven't you had enough?"

"You know what I like about remote controls, Robin?" asked Control Freak. "If you don't like what's happening, you can change the channel."

The villain pointed his remote at the Titans.

He pressed a big button on the bottom.

The whole area exploded with blinding white light.

The Teen Titans gasped and moaned, rubbing the dazzling flares from their eyes.

When their vision returned, they were amazed and alarmed to find themselves in a brightly colored place filled with sparkling, cartoony vegetation.

Robin held up his staff. "Where has Control Freak's remote transported us this time?"

Raven peered around at the candy cane bushes and lollipop flowers. "Oooh," she said.

"It is certainly somewhere beautiful," said Starfire.

Raven's eyes shone with wonder. "Aaah," she breathed.

"Uh," said Cyborg, "you okay, Raven?"

Raven clasped her hands together, gaping at the gumdrop trees and cotton candy bushes. "Gaah," she sighed.

"Did you hit your head?" Beast Boy asked.

"Do you know where we are?" whispered Raven.

Control Freak's giant head appeared in the sky above the Titans. "I do!" he said. "I've transported you all into the newest episode of *Pretty, Pretty Pegasus!*"

"Thank you so much!" Raven called up to Control Freak. "It's a dream come true."

Control Freak grinned. "It'll be a nightmare, because if you can't discover the way out, you'll be trapped here forever."

"Really?" squealed Raven, thrilled. "Forever?"

"Yes, forever!" replied Control Freak. "You'll be stuck with the pegasuses...." He scratched his orange hair. "Pegasi? What's the plural of pegasus?"

"A flerd," answered Raven. "It's half flock, half herd."

Control Freak rolled his eyes. "Holy smokes, you're a nerd," he said. "I'm out." His huge floating head vanished from view.

Robin peered at a shrub of gumdrops. "We have to get out of here, fast," he said. "This place is a breeding ground for cavities."

"But how?" Starfire asked.

Beast Boy turned into a dopey-looking pony. "It's a horse show," he explained. "So we probably have to hold hands and talk about the power of friendship or something stupid."

Robin reached out for his teammates' hands. "It's worth a shot."

Starfire held Robin's hand. Beast Boy held Starfire's and Raven's. Raven held Cyborg's. Cyborg held Robin's, too.

"You're my friend," Robin said warmly to Cyborg.

Cyborg smiled. "You're my friend, too."

Beast Boy grinned. "We're all friends," he gushed.

"I like the friends," said Starfire.

CHAPTER 3

Robin waited a moment, peering around at their extra-cheerful surroundings.

Nothing happened.

Robin dropped Starfire's and Cyborg's hands in disgust. "We're still here," he complained. "You guys aren't being friendly enough."

"Surely I am being the friendly!" retorted Starfire.

Cyborg pointed a furious finger at her. "I'm being way friendly!" he yelled. Then he swung his finger to point at Beast Boy. "This is his fault!"

"You're crazy," said Beast Boy. "I invented friendship!"

Beast Boy, Robin, Cyborg, and Starfire argued with one another about who was a good friend or a bad friend.

Finally, Raven couldn't take it anymore. "Guys!" she screamed.

Her teammates froze to look at her.

"This is not acceptable behavior in King Jellybean's candy kingdom," Raven scolded.

Cyborg nodded, his mechanical eye twinkling. "You're right," he said. "Marshal Marshmallow might throw us into the Peppermint Prison."

"Thank you, Cyborg," said Raven.

Cyborg looked surprised. "Is that a real guy?" he asked. "I was trying to make fun of you."

Raven covered her forehead with her hand. "Look," she said. "This world may seem ridiculous to you, but these cotton candy bushes have gotten me through some dark times. Now, c'mon, if anyone can help us, it's Butterbean and Sparkleface."

She led her teammates through the sugary world, following the candy path until they saw the flerd's village up ahead.

The Teen Titans approached the village cautiously, not wanting to alarm its sweet inhabitants.

Raven felt more and more nervous and excited the closer to the village they walked. "Oh my gosh," she said when she saw Butterbean and Sparkleface in the village. "There they are! I have to talk to them." She started to run ahead, but Robin jumped in her way.

"Wait, Raven," warned Robin. "Making contact with fictional characters could permanently alter their reality."

"Perhaps Beast Boy can disguise himself as the pegasus?" suggested Starfire.

"Sorry," replied Beast Boy. "I don't do mythological creatures."

Cyborg slapped him on the back. "Bro, it's just a horse with bird wings," he said. "You can do it."

Beast Boy looked unsure. "I guess I could give it a shot," he said. He closed his eyes and concentrated hard, straining to use his powers in a way they were never meant to be used.

The Titans stepped back as Beast Boy popped into the form of a half-horse, half-bird creature. He was horrifyingly ugly, with a bird beak on a horse head, bird wings, two skinny legs, a long tail, and patchy feathers.

Beast Boy collapsed onto the ground, unable to walk or fly in his newly misshaped body. He crawled a little before flopping down again. "Dude, this is agony," he moaned. "Like pulling a muscle and having brain freeze at the same time."

"Just go talk to them," Robin ordered.

Slowly, painfully, Beast Boy dragged himself into the village.

In the middle of their settlement, Butterbean and Sparkleface pondered the harsh music that thumped in the distance.

"Maybe if we give the unicorns juice and cookies they will stop playing their loud music," said Butterbean.

"That's a great idea, Butterbean," said Sparkleface.

They both gasped when they saw Beast Boy crawling into the clearing.

"Hello, friends," groaned Beast Boy. His mishmash of a body collapsed in miserable exhaustion.

Sparkleface and Butterbean screamed.

CHAPTER 4

Hiding in the bushes with Robin, Cyborg, and Starfire, Raven listened to Butterbean and Sparkleface scream. "This isn't working," said Raven worriedly.

"Just give Beast Boy some time," replied Robin. "He knows what he's doing."

But Beast Boy kept moaning in agony, and

Butterbean and Sparkleface kept screaming in total terror.

"I can't take this," Raven said. "I've got to talk to them."

She pushed out of the bushes and floated over to Butterbean and Sparkleface. She couldn't help giving them each a big hug. "This is amazing!" she squealed. "You guys are even fluffier in person."

Butterbean and Sparkleface gaped at the Titans. "Who are you?" Butterbean asked.

"My name is Raven," said the half demon. She waved her hand at her teammates. "These are my friends."

Sparkleface shook her glittering mane. "Would you like to be part of our flerd?" she asked.

"Uh, yes!" replied Raven.

Butterbean danced happily on her hooves. "Then let's sing the friendship song!"

Robin stepped in front of Raven. "Absolutely not," he said. "We need your help to find our way home."

"We'd love to help you," said Sparkleface, "but we're having a very big problem with our unicorn neighbors." She cocked her ear to listen to the violent sounds in the air. "They won't turn down their loud music."

"Have you not tried punching their faces?" asked Starfire.

Sparkleface and Butterbean glanced at each other in confusion.

"That's not a way to make friends," said Sparkleface.

Robin groaned. "We're wasting time here," he growled. "We have to find a way out!"

"Maybe this *is* the way out," Raven argued. "What if Control Freak put us in the episode to help them solve their problems and learn a lesson?"

"Learn a lesson?" repeated Robin, considering. "That does sound like the MO of that black-hearted couch potato."

"Take us to the unicorns," Starfire said to Sparkleface and Butterbean.

Cyborg vaulted onto Sparkleface's back. "Giddyup!" he shouted.

Sparkleface buckled under Cyborg's crushing weight. "Why would you do that?" she cried.

"I just thought maybe you could give me a ride?" said Cyborg apologetically.

Sparkleface wept big tears. "My spine feels like a thousand broken promises," she sobbed.

CHAPTER 5

After Sparkleface recovered, the flerd and the Titans made their way across the bright and sweet landscape to the unicorn castle. The wild music got louder as they got closer to the castle's towers.

They sneaked up to the castle and peered through a low window. Inside was a wide room with the unicorns Buttermilk Biscuit and Jelly Roll dancing in the middle, clip-clopping their hooves on the stones while tooting music out their horns. A unicorn named High Step stood in a DJ booth, mixing music on a turntable. Powerful sound waves echoed out of the room.

"Okay, Titans, here's the plan," whispered Robin. "I'll incapacitate them with some tear gas. Cyborg, you hit them with your sonic cannon—"

"No," Raven interrupted. "That's not how the flerd solves problems. We need to talk to them and work this out together, so we can all be friends."

Robin rolled his eyes. "Fine," he said. He hissed to Cyborg, "But if things go south…"

Cyborg nodded, readying the sonic cannon built into his hand.

Raven walked up to the castle's front door and knocked politely.

It only took a second for a unicorn to open it. "Hello," said Buttermilk Biscuit. "May I help you?"

"We were hoping you would keep the music down a little bit?" asked Raven.

Buttermilk Biscuit smiled but shook his head no. "I'm afraid we can't do that, friend."

Butterbean stepped up beside Raven. "I'm

glad you agree we are friends," she said, "but—"

Robin stepped in front of Butterbean. "Please," he said. "We'll handle this." He raised a clenched fist. "Titans, go!" he hollered, rolling a canister of tear gas into the castle.

The other Titans followed Robin as he rushed inside. As he passed Buttermilk Biscuit, Robin whacked the unicorn with his bo staff.

High Step, still wearing his DJ earphones, rushed over to help, but Beast Boy transformed into an elephant and slapped the unicorn back with his trunk.

Starfire flew around the room, zooming down at Jelly Roll. She fired an eye blast at his horn.

"My horn!" screeched Jelly Roll as the blast melted it.

Cyborg hurdled over the DJ booth, smashing all the musical equipment into a pile of rubble.

Afraid of all the violence, Butterbean and Sparkleface huddled in the doorway.

"That was scary," said Sparkleface.

"Very scary," Butterbean agreed. "But...it made the unicorns stop playing their music."

Raven rushed into the room to help the bashed unicorns. "I'm so sorry!" she said.

"What's wrong with you guys?" cried Buttermilk Biscuit. He had a big lump on his head where Robin whacked him.

"You never even tried talking to us," complained Jelly Roll. "Use your words."

"But you said you weren't going to turn down the music," argued Robin.

"The loud beats from our horns were the only things that kept the Gumdrop Goblin from leaving his cave and eating all the candy," Buttermilk Biscuit explained.

"Oooh," said Beast Boy.

"Yeah," said Cyborg. "Gotcha."

Outside the castle, the angry hollering of the Gumdrop Goblin echoed across the land.

"Oh no!" cried Butterbean. "He's going to be here any moment!"

Starfire peered worriedly at Jelly Roll's melted horn. "Can you not drop the beats with one less horn?"

"We get our strength by playing together

75

in harmony," said Buttermilk Biscuit.

Jelly Roll went a little cross-eyed as he tried to look up at his melted horn. "Maybe I can still play," he said hopefully. He tried to blow through it, but it made a horrible *blat* sound.

"My ears!" yelled Beast Boy.

Jelly Roll blushed in embarrassment and began to weep. "It's not working," he sobbed.

The other unicorns all started to cry, too.

Robin leaped up to Buttermilk Biscuit. He slapped the unicorn in the face. "Get it together!" he shouted. Then he slapped High Step. "Snap out of it!" Robin backhanded Jelly Roll. "Get your horns in the game!"

Jelly Roll gave Robin a hurt look and tilted his melted horn.

"Oh, sorry," said Robin. He opened his

arms to everyone in the room. "We need to focus on the problem at hand!"

Buttermilk Biscuit tossed his mane. "You're right," he said. "I don't know what came over us."

Sparkleface and Butterbean stared at Robin in awe.

"Those slaps worked really well," said Butterbean.

Sparkleface nodded. "I liked watching it."

CHAPTER 6

The Teen Titans, the unicorns, and the flerd gathered in the grassy square outside the castle to wait for the Gumdrop Goblin.

"That goblin's almost here," said Robin. "We need a plan."

"I say we form a friendship circle," suggested Jelly Roll, "so we can hug him from all angles and show him that he's loved and valued."

"Or…" Butterbean said, "we could kick him in the face."

"Butterbean!" gasped Raven. "What's wrong with you?"

"That just seems like the fastest way to get rid of him," replied Butterbean.

"But…" said Raven, "you taught me friendship and love are always the best ways to deal with problems."

"Did I?" answered Butterbean. "That sounds ridiculous."

"Agreed," said Robin as the Gumdrop Goblin lumbered into the town square. "Titans, go!"

Robin, Cyborg, Starfire, and Beast Boy bravely charged toward the goblin. They dropped into attack positions. Before they could fight, the Gumdrop Goblin scooped up the four Titans in his giant hand. Casually and effortlessly, he tossed them across the entire candy kingdom.

They screamed as they soared away, disappearing into the distance.

"Oh no," cried Sparkleface. "What do we do now, Raven?"

Raven set her jaw in determination. "We do what the old Butterbean and Sparkleface would have done."

"*Not* punch him in the face?" suggested Butterbean.

"Good," said Raven. "And…?"

"Have the unicorns play their music!" said Sparkleface.

"Exactly," said Raven.

Jelly Roll raised his damaged head. "But my broken horn will only make funny sounds."

"Butterbean," asked Raven, "what do you have to say about that?"

Butterbean smiled, fluttering her pretty wings. "Well, a broken horn doesn't matter if you play from your heart. Just do your best and we'll be proud of you no matter what."

"That's what I'm talking about!" Raven cheered.

The unicorns circled closer together. They began tootling their horns, making funky beats. Sparkleface, Butterbean, and Raven got into the groove while the unicorns aimed their beats up toward the giant goblin. The Gumdrop Goblin furiously started pulling candy chunks off the castle and gobbling them down.

Jelly Roll's horn didn't sound the same as before, but he adapted quickly to the new noises he could make.

The goblin seemed somewhat calmer, although he kept eating pieces of the castle.

"It's working," said Sparkleface. "But it's not enough!"

"I've got it," said Raven. She spread open her arms with a magical flourish. Swirls of dark energy circled around her, creating gigantic arms stretching out from her.

Raven turned toward the Gumdrop Goblin with her enormous arms. To the goblin's surprise, Raven wrapped her vast limbs around him and gave him a warm hug.

"I love and value you, Gumdrop Goblin," said Raven.

The goblin dropped the chunk of candy tower he was munching. A happy smile lit up his face. "That's all I needed to hear," he growled.

The Gumdrop Goblin turned around and left the square, skipping cheerfully back into the forest.

Raven's arms shrunk back down to normal. She hugged Butterbean, Sparkleface, and the unicorns. "We did it!" she cheered.

Her teammates returned from their trek across the realm, looking rather disheveled.

"Okay, let's pound some face!" Robin declared. He glanced around, searching for the goblin. "Hey, where'd he go?"

Raven gave Butterbean a meaningful wink. "We handled it," she said, "with friendship."

"And that worked?" asked Cyborg. "Huh."

"Then we solved the problem and learned the lesson," announced Starfire.

A bright white light glowed on the edges of the Titans' vision.

"We're going back home!" hooted Beast Boy.

"Good-bye!" cried Sparkleface. "We'll never forget you!"

"You'll always be part of our flerd," added Butterbean.

The white glow overwhelmed the Teen Titans, and they lost sight of Butterbean, Sparkleface, the unicorns, and the candy tower.

When their vision cleared, the Titans found themselves back in Jump City, on the street in front of the department store. Control Freak was still there, watching *Pretty, Pretty Pegasus* on the storefront TV. The episode was just ending, and Control Freak wiped his eyes, obviously emotional from the touching story.

"That was really beautiful," Control Freak said softly. "Well done, Titans."

"Hey!" Robin shouted. "It's Control Freak! Get him!"

Starfire blasted the villain with her powerful eyebeams. Beast Boy turned into a ram and head-butted Control Freak, while Cyborg shot a burst of compressed sound from his sonic cannon at the creep.

Control Freak howled as the Titans pummeled him.

Raven shook her head and sighed. Had they learned nothing?

CHAPTER 1

One sunny morning, Raven sat up in bed.
She winced and pressed her fingers against her temples. "What a headache," she groaned.

Moving gingerly, Raven floated toward the door. "I really need peace and quiet today," she murmured.

Just then, Robin leaped into the doorway.

He made a crazy face and an even stranger noise.

Raven yelped and shot backward, startled. She gasped. "What was that?"

"That, Raven," replied Robin, "was crazy!"

"Oh no," Raven said, covering her forehead with her hand. "Please don't tell me today is—"

Cyborg, Beast Boy, and Starfire also leaped into the doorway around Robin. "Crazy Day!" they cheered in unison.

"Okay," breathed Raven. "Stop right now."

Robin shook his head, grinning madly. "Not until one of us out-crazies the rest and is named the new Captain Crazy!"

Raven pushed past her teammates and floated into the living room. "You do Crazy Day every year," she said, "and I still don't know what the point is."

"There is no point," replied Robin, hurrying in front of her. "Isn't that…"

Starfire, Cyborg, and Beast Boy joined Robin in front of Raven. They all crossed their eyes and lolled their tongues. "*Craaaaaazy?*" they finished.

Robin suddenly stood up straight and crossed his arms. "But really," he said seriously, "the point is to just let off some steam. So, as the five-time reigning Captain Crazy of Crazy Day, I want everyone to show me some crazy!"

Beast Boy and Cyborg grabbed bowls heaped with sugared cereal. They started eating messily, but they weren't using spoons.

"Check it out," announced Beast Boy. "We're eating cereal with forks! *Whaaaat?*"

"How does the milk stay on the fork?" asked Cyborg. "It doesn't!"

"Look!" called Starfire. "I have the big shoes!" She hobbled across the living room in shoes much too large for her feet. "It is enough to drive one crazy!"

Raven rubbed her temples again. "Today's not the day for this," she moaned.

Beast Boy turned into a big goose. "Actually," he said, "today *is* the day for this. Crazy Day! Remember, Rave?"

"Can you all stop saying 'crazy'?" pleaded Raven.

Concerned, Starfire peered at Raven. "Why do you never participate in the competition?"

"Maybe because you guys already drive me crazy every day," Raven replied. She pivoted to return to her room. "I'm going to lie down."

Robin jumped in front of her again. "On the ceiling?" he asked.

"Crazy!" chanted Beast Boy, Cyborg, and Starfire.

Before she entered her room, Raven shook her head and grimaced. "And thanks for making my headache worse," she said.

Then she stepped inside and closed the door behind her.

CHAPTER 2

Raven floated in the middle of her chamber, trying to calm herself. "The one day I need them to not to annoy me—"

A searing blast of pain zapped through her brain. She fluttered backward, losing her balance as the world seemed to turn inside out. Spirals of kaleidoscopic color surrounded her, swirling dizzyingly.

"What's going on?" she cried.

Her body started to spin along with the whirl of colors, twirling her into its center as though she were being pulled into a black hole.

"Whoa!" Raven gasped.

Quick flashes of memories flared up around her: herself in a tranquil park by a duck pond, then lost in a canyon of flames, then atop an insanely tall tree, then floating in the dark void of outer space. Raven waved her arms and glanced around wildly, trying to make sense of it all.

"Where am I?" she whimpered.

"You are in your mind," a deep voice answered.

"Oh," said Raven. "No wonder it's so dark."

"And it's about to get darker," the voice

continued, "because I'm here to break it."

Wispy images streamed from Raven's skull out into the darkness, pictures of Butterbean and Sparkleface, scary skulls, vampire bats, candy bars, raging demons, and slices of gooey pizza.

"Cute," said Raven bravely. "But if you want to drive me crazy, you'll have to do better than that."

"Oh, don't you worry," the voice replied. "I know exactly how to drive you crazy." Its insane laughter echoed throughout her mind.

"Well," Raven said, trying not to show that she was wincing, "that laugh is kind of annoying. You got that going."

"Hmph," the voice said.

Then the world inside Raven's brain swirled again, sucking her deep into a whirling vortex of madness.

Meanwhile, her teammates huddled out-side her bedroom door, listening to the crashing sounds inside.

"The ruckus is coming from Raven's room," said Starfire.

"I know we're not allowed in there," said Robin, "but maybe we should see what's going on?"

"Are you crazy?" gasped Beast Boy.

Everyone blinked.

"Why, yes, my dear sir," replied Robin in a terrible British accent. "I am! Whoo-hoo!"

Robin turned the knob and pushed open the door to Raven's room.

"Raven...?" Cyborg asked as they entered.

They looked up to find Raven lying flat against the ceiling.

"Sorry, Raven is not here," a deep, frightening voice replied out of Raven's mouth. "I have taken over her mind and body."

The Titans all shuddered. That voice was creepy!

Then Robin rubbed his chin. "Lying on the ceiling," he mused. "Talking in a crazy voice..."

"She's doing it," said Cyborg. "She's going after your crazy crown!"

"Crazy voices rule!" cheered Beast Boy. He deepened his own voice and made it scratchy.

"Beast Boy is not here, either." He laughed in delight.

"She said she did not want to be crazy on Crazy Day," said Starfire, "but she is the craziest of us all."

"Oh, thank you," said the voice, sounding pleased. "I *have* been called the Lord of Madness from time to time."

CHAPTER 3

Inside the wild whirlpool of her mind, Raven watched her teammates chat with her body on the ceiling. "Ugh," she groaned. "What's wrong with them?" She shook her head and told the voice, "If they haven't driven me crazy yet, there's not much hope for you."

"Don't give up on them just yet, Raven," the voice said.

"What's that supposed to mean?" Raven asked, suspicious.

"You'll see," the voice teased. "Now...if you want me, come and get me."

A thick, soupy fog swirled around Raven until she lost all sense of direction in the haze.

"Oooh," she said, sounding both sarcastic and a little scared. "This is *so* mysterious. It feels like my mind is breaking."

Raven wandered through the fog. How long she walked in the mists...she had no idea.

Eventually, she reached a clearing. Inside was a huge sphinx, a creature with the body of a lion, the wings of an eagle, and the face of Starfire.

"Halt!" demanded the Starfire Sphinx.

"What are you supposed to be?" asked Raven.

The Starfire Sphinx ignored Raven's question. "To pass me the by and go the way, the answer to my riddle you must say."

"Go for it," said Raven. "I love riddles."

The Starfire Sphinx cleared her throat. "What is running and walks, and with a mouth and talks, and has a head and also a bed?" she asked.

Raven squinted at her. "What?"

"Oooh," the Starfire Sphinx chirped nervously, "did I misspoken the riddle?"

"Yeah," Raven replied. "You definitely misspokened it."

"I will try again," the Starfire Sphinx said. "Ahem. What runs with its head to its bed, and a mouth is having, and does not walk?"

Raven rolled her eyes. "Really?"

The Starfire Sphinx screwed up her face in concentration. "What has a bed in its mouth and is talking, but also not walking to his head?" she tried again.

"You're starting to drive me crazy," Raven complained.

Behind Raven, a scary crack zigzagged in the wall of fog. There was no damage to the fog itself, but instead to Raven's entire interior reality.

The Starfire Sphinx looked insulted. "This is a very difficult riddle," she pouted.

"That's the point," Raven seethed. She let out a little hiccup of frustration, and a chunk of the ground fell into a bottomless pit below. Raven gazed down into the hole beside her and took a deep breath, calming herself. She even smiled a little. "I'm sorry," Raven told the Starfire Sphinx. "Just take your time and try to remember what the riddle is about."

"Well, I-I—" the Starfire Sphinx stammered.

"Do you even know what the answer is?" asked Raven.

"Of course I do!" the Starfire Sphinx said indignantly.

"Yeah, right," Raven scoffed.

"It is the river, Raven!" declared the Starfire Sphinx.

"Cool," said Raven. "The answer is a river."

The Starfire Sphinx's lion shoulders slumped. "You may pass," she said sadly.

Raven smiled as she strolled past and back into the fog beyond.

109

CHAPTER 4

In the Titans Tower living room, Raven sat cross-legged on the ceiling, hanging upside down. "You think that's crazy?" the deep voice asked out of her mouth. "Watch this!"

She clapped her hands and a patterned lamp shade appeared on her head. "How do you like my hat?" the voice asked.

"Ray-ray so cray-cray!" said Beast Boy.

Starfire grinned. "That is not even the hat!"

Cyborg nudged Robin with his metallic elbow. "I think I know who our new Captain Crazy is going to be."

Robin spun to face his teammates. "No way!" he insisted angrily. "I refuse to let Raven be the craziest on Crazy Day!" *C'mon, Robin*, he scolded himself. *You have to up your game.* He started to slap himself hard on the face as the other Titans watched in concern.

"The Crazy Day is supposed to be fun, Robin," said Starfire softly.

"Yeah, dude," agreed Beast Boy, turning into a chicken. "You're starting to scare us."

"You're acting kind of crazy," added Cyborg.

"Good!" screamed Robin. "But not crazy enough!" He gasped out deep, ragged breaths. "Time for some crazy training!"

While a bizarre song blasted throughout the Tower, Robin ran around performing crazy exercises. First he did a set of push-*downs* instead of push-*ups*, pulling himself toward the floor.

"Robin's push-downs make none of the sense," exclaimed Starfire.

Then Robin made the craziest straw ever to be called a crazy straw, with dozens of twists and loops. He poked one end into a big glass of milk and got slurping.

"That is one crazy straw, bro!" bleated Beast Boy, who had changed into a goat. "How many loops is the milk going to go through?"

Instead of replying, Robin rushed out to buy dozens of televisions. Then he sold them for a deep discount.

"What's wrong with him?" demanded

Cyborg. "He can't afford to sell those TVs at such low prices. He must be crazy!"

As the song faded out, Robin flexed his arms, showing the results of all his training. His biceps popped up on the underside of his arms. "Crazy!" he declared.

Meanwhile, inside her mind, Raven was still lost in the mists. She stumbled through the murk for what felt like weeks.

Finally, the smoke cleared, revealing a giant chessboard.

As Raven walked closer, she could see that the pieces were life-size. In fact, the rook was shaped like an elephant—it was Beast Boy. And the knight next to him was Cyborg!

Raven rolled her eyes, already over this chess thing. "So what are you two supposed to be?"

"We sort of, like, challenge you to a game or whatever," said Beast Boy.

"Yes," added Cyborg dramatically. "It is a game of checkers...to the death!"

"This is actually chess, not checkers," said Raven.

Beast Boy shrugged, which looked odd on an elephant. "What's the difference?"

"Ugh," said Raven, rubbing her temples again.

When she had calmed herself, Raven stared out at the chessboard, deciding what to do. After considering many opening moves, Raven conjured up a giant magic arm that picked up a black pawn and moved it forward two squares.

"Your move," she told Beast Boy and Cyborg.

They blinked blankly at her.

"What?" asked Beast Boy.

Cyborg peered down at the marble horse he was sitting atop. "You want us to move?"

"Yeah," Raven replied.

CHAPTER 5

Beast Boy and Cyborg waited a moment, and then they began to dance. Mostly they just wiggled their arms and tilted their heads, since they couldn't really move their marble bases enough to dance.

"We're movin'," said Beast Boy, getting into the groove.

"Uh-huh!" said Cyborg, moving his head

like a pigeon to the rhythm. "That's right! Woo!"

Raven glared at them. Cracks in the inner reality formed behind her as she teetered on the edge of losing control.

"Hey," Raven demanded. "Are you kidding me? How can chess pieces not know how to play chess?"

"We've never been chess pieces till now," replied Cyborg. His voice got oddly deeper halfway through his sentence.

"How can I win if you don't know how to play?" growled Raven.

"Dude," said Beast Boy, "that's a good question."

"And the answer is she *can't* win, bro!" cheered Cyborg. "Which means we can't lose!"

Beast Boy pumped his fist. "Are we about to win our very first game of chess? Awesome!"

"I'd high-five you if I could reach you," said Cyborg.

Raven pressed her palms against her temples, as though trying to keep her head from exploding. *Can't let them drive me crazy*, she scolded herself. She looked up at Cyborg and Beast Boy. "Go ahead," she told them. "Celebrate."

"She's right," said Beast Boy. "This moment is too beautiful not to commemorate."

"If we can't high-five, then let's high-forehead," Cyborg suggested.

They both began rocking back and forth, wiggling their heavy marble bases closer.

"Almost there," Cyborg grunted. "Bro…"

Beast Boy rocked a bit too hard. He wobbled, lurched, and tipped over, smacking his head right into Cyborg's.

"Ow, dummy!" cried Cyborg. Cyborg toppled over, falling into the bishop, which fell into the queen, which whacked into the king. The king hit the board with a loud thump.

Raven pumped her fist in the air. "You surrendered your king," she said. "I win."

The chessboard vanished into the fog.

When she turned around, a gigantic door loomed ahead of Raven. She marched toward it, feeling smaller as she got closer.

As she reached the door, Raven saw that the low, brass doorknob was shaped just like Robin's face.

"You would be the last obstacle," Raven told the doorknob.

"That's right, Raven," said Robin's brass face. "No one drives you crazier than I do.

122

Now if you want to pass you must…answer a riddle!"

"I've already done that," said Raven.

CHAPTER 6

"Oh," said the doorknob shaped like Robin's face. "In that case...you have to win a game of chess!"

Raven raised her eyebrows. "I did that, too."

"Really?" Robin asked. "Well, then...you have to...uh..." The doorknob let out a deep sigh. "Oh, never mind. Come on in."

Raven grabbed the doorknob and turned it.

"Ow!" cried Robin, sounding muffled under her hand. "My nose!"

The door swung open, and Raven stepped into the dark chamber beyond.

Weirdly cheerful music echoed along the arched ceiling high above. Raven walked into the darkness, heading for a faint spot of light on the other side of the room. It was an open doorway. Raven walked faster.

As she got closer, Raven stopped short, glaring in anger, now able to see into the lit room.

"You," she said.

In a cozy little den, her father, Trigon, the demon conqueror of multiple dimensions and enslaver of civilizations, sat in a comfy recliner, watching TV and eating popcorn.

"Hi, honey," said Trigon. "Lose your mind yet?"

Raven covered one eye with her hand. "Using imagery of my friends to drive me crazy," she said. "Was all this about turning me evil?"

"Got me!" chortled Trigon. He popped a piece of popcorn into his mouth and chomped on it. "Did it work?"

"Of course not," Raven replied. "I already spend every day with them. You could never drive me as crazy as they do."

"Oh, I don't know," said Trigon, leaning back in his recliner. "They actually seem pretty fun."

"Then you should spend more time with them," said Raven. Before her father could react, Raven recited her most powerful incantation. "*Azarath Metrion Zinthos!*"

Ghostly moving images of Robin, Starfire, Cyborg, and Beast Boy appeared floating in the air in a flash of magic. Raven waved her hand and then made a fist. The wisps of the Titans swirled together for a moment, then darted right into Trigon's ear.

Trigon's eyes bugged out. "Hey!" he cried. "Why'd you do that?"

Raven moved back as Trigon leaped out of his recliner. He hopped around wildly, smacking his claw against his pointy ear. But no matter how hard he whacked himself, he couldn't dislodge the spirits of the Teen Titans.

"They sure are loud!" Trigon hollered. "Stop that," he whined. "Stop calling me *bro*! I do not wish to train! You're all driving me crazy!"

Trigon shrieked a bloodcurdling scream of torment, and then vanished in a puff of smoke.

Raven smiled.

She opened her eyes.

She was in the Titans Tower living room, hovering in front of the couch.

Her teammates were watching her carefully.

"What are you looking at?" she asked.

"The new Captain Crazy," replied Robin. "Congratulations."

Raven's teammates applauded wildly.

Raven shook her head, holding up her hand for them to be quiet. "No," she said. "You don't get it. I'm not crazy. I mean, you all drive me crazy, all the time. But you know what? In the end, that's what keeps me sane."

The Titans remained silent for a second, processing Raven's words.

"That makes no sense," said Beast Boy.

"Crazy day," said Raven.

BONUS ACTIVITY!

Raven is casting spells! Write the magic words Raven uses for her spell, then draw something peculiar appearing out of her spell book.

Read all the
TEEN TITANS GO! books.